For my mother

tiger tales
an imprint of ME Media, LLC
202 Old Ridgefield Road, Wilton, CT 06897
Published in the United States 2005
Originally published as *Het geheim van IJsje* in Belgium 2004
By Uitgeverij Clavis, Amersterdam-Hasselt
Copyright © Uitgeverij Clavis, Amersterdam-Hasselt
Adapted into the English language by Sarah Prial
Printed in China
All rights reserved
1 3 5 7 9 10 8 6 4 2

Library of Congress Cataloging-in-Publication Data

Genechten, Guido van.
  [Geheim van IJsje. English]
  Snowy's special secret / by Guido van Genechten.
      p. cm.
  First published in Belgium by Uitgeverij Clavis Amsterdam-Hasselt,
2004, under the title: *Het geheim van IJsje.*
  Summary: Snowy the polar bear wants to show his mother that he loves
her more than anything else in the world by making a special gift for her,
but to do that, he has to sneak away every chance he gets.
  ISBN 1-58925-049-4 (hardcover)
  [1. Mother and child—Fiction. 2. Surprise—Fiction. 3. Gifts—Fiction.
4. Polar bear—Fiction. 5. Bears—Fiction.] I. Title.
  PZ7.G2912Sn 2005
  [E]—dc22
                                                    2004019503

Snowy's Special Secret

by Guido van Genechten

tiger tales

Snowy loved his mommy more
than anything in the world and he
wondered how he could show her.

One day, Snowy thought of a terrific surprise for her. But it was hard to keep a secret from Mommy. She always took Snowy on her daily trip to the fishing hole. So he had to make up excuses to go off on his own every once in a while to work on the surprise.

Some days Mommy was so busy fishing that she didn't notice if Snowy disappeared for a few minutes. But most days, Snowy had to think of a reason to leave her for little while.

"I dropped my toy. I'd better go back and get it"
Snowy said, as Mommy was reeling in a fish.
"Okay, but don't be gone too long, " Mommy said.

Snowy ran off as fast as he could to work on
his special secret.

When he came back to the fishing hole, Mommy was packing up to walk back home. She said to him, "That took you a very long time."

"I, um, my toy, got stuck in the snow," Snowy told her.

"I'm going out to play," Snowy said as soon as they got home that afternoon.

"Okay," said Mommy. "But come back as soon as you hear me call you for dinner."

Snowy ran off again as fast as he could.

When Mommy called Snowy in for dinner, he arrived out of breath and completely covered in snow.

"I fell down the hill," Snowy said, and he smiled as sweetly as he could.

After dinner Snowy slipped out again.
He needed just a little more time before
he could share his secret with Mommy.

Finally, the surprise was complete. Snowy ran back home to get Mommy.

"Mommy, Mommy!" he called. "Come out and look! I have something special to show you!"

Mommy's mouth dropped open when she saw the surprise. She had never seen anything so beautiful and special.

"Look Mommy! It's us!" Snowy said proudly.
Mommy gave Snowy a very big hug.

Snowy was happy that he had
surprised Mommy, and Mommy
was happy with her surprise.
"I love you," Mommy and
Snowy said to each other,
and they watched the stars
until they fell asleep.